The TREASURE TREE

The TREASURE TREE

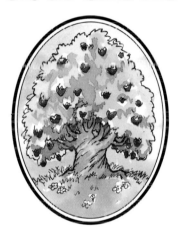

JOHN & CINDY TRENT   GARY & NORMA SMALLEY

illustrated by JUDY LOVE

WORD PUBLISHING

Dallas·London·Vancouver·Melbourne

To the very best friends in our homes—
our children:
Kari Lorraine and Laura Catherine
Kari Lynn, Gregory Thomas, and Michael Thomas
—THE TRENTS AND SMALLEYS

To Alan, Matt, and Tom
who have gone through so much with me in this work.
And to June and Opa
for their love and encouragement.
—JUDY LOVE

Managing Editor: Laura Minchew   Project Editor: Beverly Phillips

Library of Congress Cataloging-in-Publication Data

The treasure tree / John and Cindy Trent . . . [et al.] ; illustrated by Judy Love
        p.   cm.
        "Word kids."
        Summary: Four animal friends trying to get to a treaure find that their different personalities make each of them a valuable member of the search team and that the very best treaure is knowing how much they love and need each other..
        ISBN 0–8499–0936–8
        [1. Animals—Fiction. 2. Treasure hunts—Fiction. 3. Individuality—Fiction.
4. Friendship—Fiction.] I. Trent, John T.   II. Love, Judy, 1953–   ill.
PZ7.T6896 1992
[E]—dc20

92–17302
CIP
AC

Printed in the United States of America

2 3 4 5 6 7 8 9 RRD 9 8 7 6 5 4 3 2

A MESSAGE TO PARENTS FROM JOHN AND GARY

This is the story of four best friends who find out how much they need each other. And if you'll look closely, it's also the story of four different personalities and why they are each special in their own way.

In our own homes, and in the homes of hundreds of people across the country, we've seen how beneficial it can be when family members understand each other's personality strengths. The animals you'll meet in this book can teach you and your child how important each personality trait is.

As an added feature, we've included a personality checklist just so you can help your child see his or her own personality traits better. When you and your child read this story and do the checklist, we think you will begin to see not only yourselves but family and friends in a different light. Do they lean toward being a Lion, Otter, Golden Retriever, or Beaver?

So if life seems like a zoo around your house at times, or worse, like "Wild Kingdom," don't despair. There's hope. When you begin to understand each family member's unique personality strengths—especially the children's—you've gained a powerful tool to help you have the close-knit family you've always wanted.

CONTENTS

THE
BIGGEST
BIRTHDAY PARTY
EVER

Chapter One

All the forest animals had gathered for the biggest, bestest birthday party ever. There were four birthday cakes and four places of honor. And four best friends were sitting in those special places, all cheering and laughing!

There was Lance the Lion, wearing a red party hat. He always walked and talked like he was in charge.

Next to him, with a purple hat on, was Honey the Golden Retriever. Her friendly brown eyes and caring ways made others feel all toasty warm inside.

2

To Honey's right was Chewy the Beaver. He was wearing a shiny yellow hat. Chewy always wanted to do things just right. He was measuring just how wide to cut the pieces of his cake. "There's a right way to cut this cake," he said. "And that's the way I'm going to do it!"

Standing in the chair next to Chewy was Giggles the
Otter. Giggles was wearing a hat with orange polka dots on
it. She seemed to add fun and spice to every meeting of the
friends. "Watch this!" she called out, as she tossed her piece
of cake high into the air. "No hands!"

It was an expert throw. But unfortunately the cake didn't make an expert landing. It fell right on the Otter's nose, covering her face with icing! Everyone laughed and laughed at the sight of Giggles covered with icing. Then it was time to open the presents.

The last present was from the Wise Old Owl, and it was to all four of the best friends.

Lance, Giggles, Honey, and Chewy were very excited as they tore open the big package. Finally after digging through all the paper (and having to help Giggles out of the box which she had fallen in), they found something on the very bottom.

"It's a map!" said Giggles.

"Ooooh, I love maps!" said Chewy.

In fact, it was a very old map with four strange riddles. It was Honey who read out loud what the words said:

Follow this map and find four keys
That open the gate to the Treasure Tree!

To find the first key, this rule is law:
You'll have to search to the very last straw.

Key number two is by the sea,
Hidden away where none can see.

For the third treasure key, here's the rhyme:
Listen with your heart and don't waste time.

If to the Treasure Tree you want to race,
You'll have to see what's out of place.

9

"Treasure!" they all said together. "Oh, thank you, Owl!"

"Let's go!" said Lance the Lion. "I'll lead us to the Treasure Tree right now!" (Lions are always in a hurry.)

"But shouldn't we talk first about what we should do?" asked Honey the Golden Retriever.

"I haven't had time to get everything packed!" said Chewy. He was already thinking of all the things to put in his backpack.

"Hey, we haven't played any birthday games yet!" said Giggles. They all agreed to finish the party first.

Then after more yummy cake than they should have eaten in two birthdays, they decided what to do. They would start out the next morning and follow the map to find the four golden keys.

And so began four great adventures that would lead them to the Treasure Tree.

LANCE
AND THE
UNCROSSABLE
RIVER

Chapter Two

The four best friends set off through the forest to find the first golden key.

"Chewy," said Lance from his place at the front of the group. "Tell me the first clue again."

"Sure," said Chewy, who had already memorized the two short lines. (Beavers are very good at memorizing things.)
"To find the first key, this rule is law: You'll have to search to the very last straw."

12

"What do you think that means?" asked Honey.

"I don't know," said the Beaver. "The map shows we go through Blueberry Basin and across a river. Then we'll find the first treasure key!"

"Finding this key will be a piece of cake!" said Giggles the Otter.

But as you'll see, finding the key was more like a piece of pie.

13

"Here's Blueberry Basin!" announced Chewy the Beaver.

"Oh, just look!" said Honey. "It's *beautiful!*"

And it was. In fact, it looked like a small valley that had been covered by a beautiful, blue cloud.

Actually, Blueberry Basin got its name from the very special plants that grew there. Now there are many places

where patches of wild blueberries grow. But the four best
friends had never seen a patch like this. This was a
Blueberry *Pie* patch.

This was a whole valley, covered with very tall bushes
with beautiful blue leaves. And at the top of each bush grew
a delicious blueberry pie. And each pie was topped with
whipped cream! They looked so good you couldn't help
wanting to eat one.

15

"Now listen," said Lance, taking command. "We can't
reach those pies without a ladder. So let's just keep walking
and not lose time." (Lions hate to lose time. That's why it's
so hard for them to stop playing and come in for lunch!)

While Lance marched straight through Blueberry Basin,
his friends kept hopping and bouncing as they walked. They
were trying to reach one of those delicious pies.

Finally, Giggles couldn't stand it any longer. She just had
to have a blueberry pie. She called for Honey and Chewy to
huddle up and whispered her plan.

Then, without a word to Lance, they made a human
ladder. Honey got on Chewy's shoulders, and Giggles
climbed way up on top of Honey's shoulders! Giggles was
pulling one of the delicious pies toward her when . . .

"*Hurry!*" said Chewy the Beaver, who was starting to wobble. "I can't hold you two up much longer!"

"I've got it!" said Giggles. And she inched the top of the pie bush down closer and closer. . . . *Then suddenly Chewy's legs gave way!*

18

As the three friends tumbled to the ground, Giggles lost her grip on the pie.

"WHOOSH!" The bush snapped back into place. But the pie came loose and shot forward.

"Oh, no!" cried the three friends, when they saw where the pie was headed. *"Look out, Lance!"*

"PLOPPP!" went the pie with a thud on Lance's head—whipped cream and all! And unlike Giggles, who *liked* having icing on her head, Lance was not happy.

Chewy, Honey, and Giggles were laughing so hard they couldn't get up. But finally they rushed to Lance.

"We're so sorry!" said Honey.

"Sorry!" said Lance with a growl. But then a big grin spread across his face.

"I'm not sorry! This pie is *terrrrrrrrrrific!"*

And as they helped Lance clean up, they also helped themselves to the best, finger-lickinest blueberry pie they had ever eaten!

"All right," said Lance, finally looking more like a Lion than a blueberry. "Let's get moving toward the river!" In no time they reached the river. But the minute they saw it, they knew they had a big problem.

It was the widest, meanest, deepest, and coldest river in all the forest!

21

"How can we get across?" Honey the Golden Retriever wanted to know. "There are no boats or bridges. How can we find the treasure key if we can't get across the river?

"I have an idea," said Chewy the Beaver, pulling out his pocket calendar and calculator. "Let's wait right here until the river freezes over. Let's see. . . . That's just about 180 days! Then we'll be able to walk across!"

"Great idea!" said Giggles. "That'll give us plenty of time to eat some more pie!"

"But we can't wait that long!" said Honey. "What if someone else finds the treasure key before we do!"

Being such a good leader, Lance the Lion already had a plan. "I'll tell you what we're going to do!" said Lance.

"If a pie can fly through the air and hit me on the head, then we ought to be able to fly through the air to get across the river!"

"But how?" asked Honey.

"No time for questions!" said Lance. "Just do what I say!"

Without further discussion, Lance ran over to the water's edge and selected a strong, young tree.

"When I bend this tree down, I want all of you to climb up on top of it—*now!*"

Lance had bent the young tree almost to the ground. With doubting looks, the three friends all climbed up on top of the tree.

"Here we go!" shouted Lance the Lion,
as he jumped up with the others. Then
"SWOOOOOOSH!" The tree flung them
high in the air and all the way across the river—
right onto a haystack!

26

"What a ride!" said Giggles!

"Boy, I'll say!" said Chewy the Beaver, looking at his watch. "We were in the air for fourteen seconds before we hit this haystack."

"HAYSTACK!" they all shouted at the same time, remembering the first riddle.

"To find the first key, this rule is law:
You'll have to search to the very last straw."

"Haystacks are made of straw!" said Lance. Quickly all four friends began digging in the haystack to find the first golden key.

They searched all the way to the very bottom of the haystack. And there it was, a beautiful, golden key . . . attached to the *very last straw*.

"We found it!" they cried.

One key was now theirs because of a Lion's quick thinking and determined personality. But three other keys and three exciting adventures lay between them and the Treasure Tree. And the next adventure would be the scariest of all.

"Good people are as brave as a lion."—PROVERBS

GIGGLES
AND THE
CRYSTAL COVE
CLAM

Chapter Three

Now the four best friends were eager to find the second key. So off they went to Crystal Cove, the next stop on the map.

"Are we *really* going all the way to the ocean?" Honey asked excitedly. "I've never been to the beach!"

"I haven't either!" said Giggles. "I can't wait to build sandcastles . . . and play with a beach ball . . . and go for a walk with a crab . . . and shake hands and hands and hands with an octopus . . . and jump in the water and . . ."

"Wait a minute!" said Chewy. "Remember we're looking for the treasure key, not a playground. The map says: *'Key number two is by the sea, hidden away where none can see.'*"

"That's right," said Lance. "Look, there's the ocean!"

The four best friends stopped as they came out of the forest. Down below them they could see the beautiful, blue waters of Crystal Cove. To the right, a steep trail led down to the beach.

"Let's go!" shouted Lance. And he started down the trail with the other animals right behind him.

Giggles was last in line going down the steep trail. She was looking at the beautiful water far away and not watching where she was going. That's why she tripped right over the big seashell.

What happened next was like pushing over a row of dominoes. Giggles fell into Chewy the Beaver, who fell into Honey the Golden Retriever, who fell into Lance the Lion!

"*Whoooaaa!*" they cried. But no one could stop. Spinning faster and faster, they rolled together down the hill like big, colorful balls. Then PLOP-P-P-P! They landed right on their heads in the sand!

"That was great! shouted Giggles, getting up with a smile and brushing the sand from her clothes. "Let's do it again!"

"Well, I guess that tumble did get us to the beach quicker," said Chewy. "Now we're even ahead of schedule!"

"Is anybody hurt?" asked Honey.

"I'll tell you who's going to be hurting if I catch her!" said Lance with a smile, chasing after Giggles in a playful game of tag.

Then Honey reminded them they needed to look for the key . . . *hidden away where none can see.*

35

This wasn't going to be easy. After all, what you can't see can be very difficult to find. So the four animals began searching the beach at Crystal Cove for the second treasure key. Lance began jogging up and down the beach to see if he could spot a clue (and to get some exercise at the same time).

Honey and Giggles went right down to the water's edge.
Giggles played tag with a sand crab. And Honey visited a
family of sea gulls. Then suddenly they heard a horrible
scream from down the beach.

It was Chewy.

37

The Beaver had discovered a mystery. Or actually, the mystery had discovered him. As he was trying to measure just how long the beach was in Beaver feet, "Splash!" He was hit in the face with a big squirt of water.

"What was that?" he said to himself, looking around for someone who had squirted him. But the only thing nearby was a very large rock.

38

"Rocks can't squirt water!" he thought, looking at it closely.

Chewy was right. Rocks can't squirt water. But a *clam* can—especially the biggest, most gigantic clam in all of Crystal Cove. Not only can a clam squirt water, but sometimes it can do other things even more troublesome.

Chewy heard a loud "CR-R-E-E-E-E-K" like an old door with rusty hinges opening. Then . . . "SNAP!" The giant clam had opened its mouth and snapped it shut . . . *right on Chewy's tail!*

"Yeeeoooowwwww!" came the Beaver's loud scream.

"LET GO! Get me out of here!" shouted the Beaver.

When the three friends got to Chewy, they found not
one but *two* big problems. Their best friend had his tail
caught by a giant clam, and the tide was beginning to come
in! Wave by wave the ocean was getting closer!

"I'll get him out!" cried Lance. And with all his strength,
he pushed and pulled. But nothing happened.

Honey tried to encourage Chewy. She held the Beaver's hand and said, "Don't worry. It'll all be better soon. You're being so brave. . . ."

This helped the Beaver not to be so scared . . . but it didn't open the clam's jaws.

"The water's coming closer!" shouted a very tired Lance. "We've got to think of another way to get the clam's jaws open!"

"I know how to get the clam to open its mouth!" the hopeful Otter said.

"How?" said the others.

"I'll tell him some of my jokes. And then when he's laughing, Chewy can get his tail free!"

"*Jokes?* . . . At a time like this?" said Chewy.

"*Trust me,*" Giggles said. "I know lots of jokes, but I'll use only my very *best* jokes on this clam."

The Otter's friends rolled their eyes and shook their heads. But Giggles started telling her "best" jokes. (Just be thankful you aren't reading a story where she shared her "worst" jokes!)

"All right, Clam, what side of a rabbit has the most fur? . . . The right side? . . . The left side? . . . No, it's the *outside!*" she said, bursting into laughter. But not even a chuckle came from the clam.

"Okay, okay. How about this one? . . . What is the most musical fish? . . . A *tune-a-fish*! Get it!" she said, doubling over with laughter.

"It's not working!" cried Chewy, as he watched the water coming closer.

"Not to worry," said Giggles. "This next one will work. It *always* works. . . . What happens when ducks fly upside down? . . . They *quack up!*"

At last, from deep down inside the clam shell, came a rumble. Then a chuckle shook the clam, but he did not open his mouth and laugh.

Giggles was discouraged for only a moment. Then suddenly she shouted, "I've got it now. I know what will get that old clam to open up!" And off she ran down the beach.

Quick as a flash, Giggles was back with a feather from one of the sea gulls.

Honey the loyal Golden Retriever was still by Chewy's side. But the water was getting higher. And Lance was still trying to force the clam to open his mouth.

"Stand aside!" said Giggles, holding up the feather. "This will do the trick!"

And through the little crack that was made as the clam held the Beaver's tail, the Otter stuck in the feather and began to wiggle it around.

Now, any kind of tickle can make you laugh. (In fact, you might want to try a tickle right now.) But a *feather* tickle is the most ticklish of all.

And sure enough, the clam began to chuckle, and then to laugh. And finally, the clam's mouth flew wide open, and Chewy the Beaver was free.

"HURRAY!" they all cheered.

"Look!" shouted Honey. "It's the key!"

There in the clam's mouth . . . *hidden away where none could see* . . . they found another golden key.

49

Now the four best friends were half way to the Treasure Tree. The first key was found by the Lion's quick thinking and determined personality. The second key was won by the Otter's joyful and hopeful ways. That left only two more keys. And key number three would be perhaps the hardest of all to find.

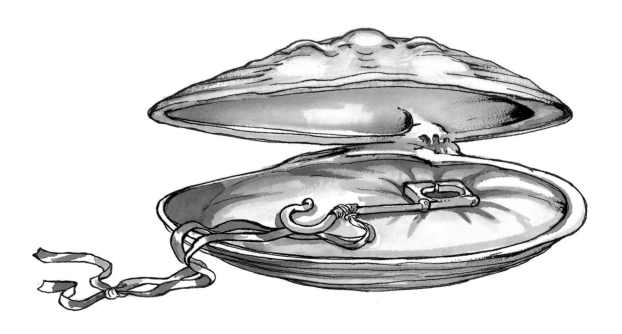

"A happy heart is like good medicine."—PROVERBS

HONEY
AND THE
ADVENTURE AT
PEPPERMINT FALLS

Chapter Four

When the four best friends came to a beautiful, grassy meadow, they stopped for a picnic. They had been so busy finding the first two keys they had almost forgotten to eat lunch.

"I'm having what I always have," said Chewy the Beaver. "A peanut butter and jelly sandwich cut in half and a carefully washed carrot for dessert."

"I'm having three Cheeseburgers and an energy shake," said Lance the Lion.

"I'm having fresh vegetables and a slice of wheat bread," said Honey the Golden Retriever.

"And I'm having what I always have," said the cheerful Otter. "At least what I always have on Tuesdays . . . cupcakes with pickle icing. And I brought plenty for everyone!"

"Yuck!" said Chewy and Honey. *"Cupcakes with pickle icing?"*

"Double Yuck!" said Lance.

"That's enough about food, we need to look at the treasure map," said Chewy. "It says right here that to find the next key, we must go to . . . go to . . . go to . . ." sputtered the Beaver.

"Go to *where?*" said the Lion impatiently.

"To Peppermint Falls!" He finally got the words out.

"Peppermint Falls!" they all cried with excitement. "Oh, let's go right now!"

Now, if you lived in the forest where the best friends did, then you'd know why they were so excited. They had heard their parents tell stories about Peppermint Falls. It was a wonderful place. Mint bushes and crystal clear water mixed together in just the right way to make the water turn into peppermint!

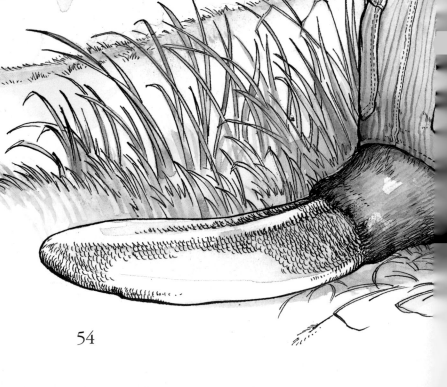

Candy canes grew everywhere. But these weren't ordinary candy canes. Even kids who don't like peppermint *love* these. They never get sticky when you lick them. They never turn your fingers red. And they don't even get lint on them if they brush against your sweater.

Chewy read them the words on the map.

"For the third treasure key, here's the rhyme: Listen with your heart and don't waste time."

"What does that mean?" asked Honey.

"Who cares!" said the others. "We're on our way to Peppermint Falls!" And so they were, and right into another big adventure.

The map showed Peppermint Falls to the north of where they were. And Chewy the Beaver knew exactly how to get there. He had brought along a compass to help find directions. (Beavers always carry extra things—a pocket knife, a flashlight, and other things like that—"just in case.")

In no time, they were headed north through the forest. As they hiked along, they were thinking of all those candy canes! And *that's* when it happened.

"*Help!*" said a very small voice, just barely above a whisper.

"*Help me!*"

"Stop!" said Honey the Golden Retriever. "Did you hear that?"

"Hear what?" said Lance, from the front of the group.

"I didn't hear anything," said Chewy, who was checking off each landmark they passed on the map.

"I can't hear very well upside down," said Giggles. The Otter was giving her feet a rest by walking on her hands just for fun.

"Well, maybe I was mistaken," said Honey. And the four best friends continued their march.

As they got closer to Peppermint Falls, the sound of rushing water became louder. But Honey's sensitive ears heard the small voice a second time.

"Help!" cried the voice. *"Somebody please help me!"*

"Did you hear it that time?" Honey asked, looking around for some sign of trouble.

"Hear *what?*" said Lance. "The waterfall?"

"No . . . someone calling for help!" said Honey.

"I think you're hearing things," said Giggles.

"The sound of the waterfall *could* be playing tricks on you," said Chewy the Beaver.

"The sound of the waterfall is making *me* hungry!" said Lance. "We're so close, you can even smell the peppermint. Come on. Let's go!" Honey was left by herself as her three friends scampered off toward Peppermint Falls.

"I just *know* I heard something," said Honey. But after searching all around and finding nothing, she ran to catch up with her friends.

In a few minutes, they got their first look at Peppermint Falls. It was breathtaking! There, shimmering in the sunlight was a high waterfall with peppermint stripes of pure milk-white and bright, Christmas red.

And right before them, all along both riverbanks grew the yummiest, sweetest, most wonderful candy canes you could imagine.

"We're here!" shouted Lance, and all four of the animals jumped around. They were almost as excited as if they had found the Treasure Tree itself.

Soon they were licking, slurping, and even chewing on the best candy they'd ever tasted. That is, all except Honey. She had heard that tiny voice again.

"Help me! There isn't much time. Please, help me!"

"Maybe I *am* hearing things," said Honey to herself. "No one else seems to hear." She could see the others already eating candy canes.

But deep in her heart, she knew someone needed her help. And she knew she couldn't waste any more time.

"That sound has to be coming from somewhere," said Honey. Quickly she looked under rocks and pushed aside bushes.

67

Finally, she saw a flash of color between two trees. Then she heard that same, small voice crying, *"Quick, help me! . . . He's coming!"*

The voice came from a beautiful butterfly, who was caught in a very large spider web. And the very large spider had just returned home for some lunch! (And butterflies were his favorite meal.)

The spider was licking his lips at the thought of a butterfly feast when "FLASH!" Honey snapped off a branch that held one side of the web. And a very surprised spider was sent tumbling into the bushes.

Very gently Honey helped free the butterfly from the strands of web.

"Thank you very much," said the beautiful butterfly. "You're welcome," said the Golden Retriever. "Would you come with me and tell my friends that I'm not hearing things?" And that's just what she did.

After hearing the butterfly's story, the three friends all cheered Honey the Golden Retriever. And that's when Chewy the Beaver remembered why they'd come up to Peppermint Falls in the first place.

"The treasure key!" said Chewy. "We've forgotten about the treasure key! . . . And that we all need to listen with our heart . . ."

"But Honey didn't forget," said the butterfly, in her sweet little voice.

"I didn't?" asked the kindhearted dog, looking a little confused.

71

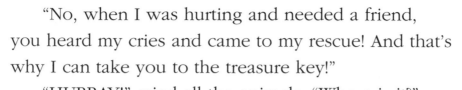

"No, when I was hurting and needed a friend,
you heard my cries and came to my rescue! And that's
why I can take you to the treasure key!"

"HURRAY!" cried all the animals. "Where is it?"

And they all followed the butterfly to a tree filled with
cocoons—all bursting forth with butterflies. And there,
hanging in the midst of the tree, was a small, golden key.

72

CHEWY

AND THE
OUT-OF-PLACE
HARES

Chapter Five

The four best friends were on their way to find key number four. As they marched together though the forest, they sang a marching song. (One you can sing, too.)

We're the four best friends you see,
And we're headed for the Treasure Tree.
Just one more little key
And the treasure we will see.

Well, they had just sung this song for the *twenty-fifth* time when they saw Aaron the Artistic Elephant! Now Aaron was one of the best-liked animals in the entire forest.

76

"Aaron the Artistic Elephant!" they all
cried. Then they ran to where he was
standing in a field of yellow flowers.

77

"Where are the four of you off to on such a fine day?" asked Aaron.

"Wise Old Owl gave us a treasure map for our birthdays!" said Honey. "And we're off to find the Treasure Tree!"

"Wonderful!" said Aaron. "I'd love to paint a picture of the Treasure Tree."

"Perhaps you can one day," said Lance. "But for now, we've got to find one more golden key that will get us in to see it."

"That's right," said Chewy. "Just listen to this last clue on our map. *If to the Treasure tree you want to race, you'll have to see what's out of place.'"

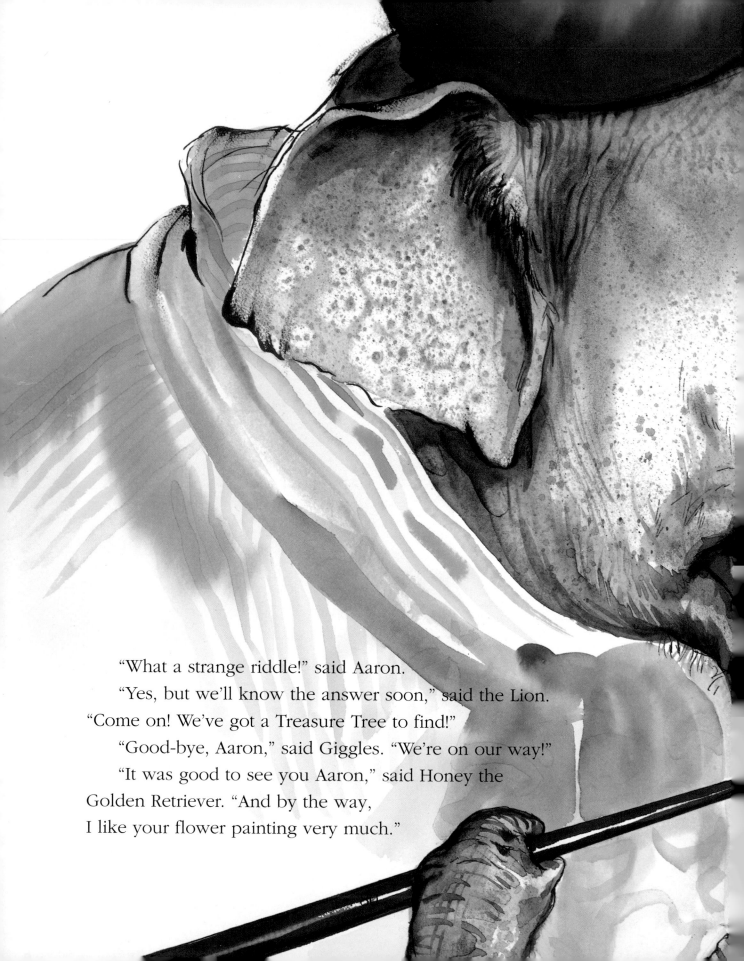

"What a strange riddle!" said Aaron.

"Yes, but we'll know the answer soon," said the Lion.
"Come on! We've got a Treasure Tree to find!"

"Good-bye, Aaron," said Giggles. "We're on our way!"

"It was good to see you Aaron," said Honey the
Golden Retriever. "And by the way,
I like your flower painting very much."

"Thank you. I've had a great deal of trouble with my paintings," said Aaron.

"But Aaron," said Honey, "your flower looks *beautiful!*"

"Oh, I haven't been having trouble *painting* a flower. I've been having trouble keeping my pictures from flying away."

"Flying away?" said Chewy. "What do you mean?"

81

"Well," said Aaron. "I'm allergic to flowers. And every time I finish a painting . . . I . . . I . . . *I . . . AH–CHOOOOOOOOOOOOOOOOOOOOOOOOOOOOOOO!*" went the elephant. And his big sneeze blew away his picture and . . . *the four friends as well!*

"Where did they go?" said Aaron looking all around, suddenly all alone.

Where they went was for an unexpected sneeze ride.
And where they landed was at Confusion Junction.

The best friends didn't know it yet, but Aaron's mighty
sneeze had landed them right where they needed to be.
Confusion Junction was a place where the main road split
into four roads.

And right where the four roads began stood four silly hares (better known as bunny rabbits).

Each rabbit had on bright blue pants, orange suspenders, a green stripped shirt, and a polka-dot bow tie! But then all four bunnies began to sing: *"Follow me. . . . Follow me. . . . I'll take you to the treasure key."*

"This is great!" said Honey the Golden Retriever. "We've got four guides to help us find the last key."

"Let's go!" said Lance the Lion.

The four friends began to walk toward the rabbits. But each rabbit ran down a *different* road, shouting all the time, *"Follow me. . . . Follow me. . . . I'll take you to the treasure key."*

"STOP!" said the friends.

86

"Which one do we follow?" said Giggles?

"They all look just alike and sound just alike, too," said Honey. "How will we *ever* find out which way to go?"

The best friends knew that only one rabbit could be right. But which one? They couldn't figure it out? Can you?

You could if you were like Chewy the Beaver.

"I know how to get to the bottom of this," said Chewy. "Remember the clue Wise Old Owl gave us? . . . *If to the Treasure Tree you want to race, you'll have to see what's **out of place.**'"

And with that, he lined up all four bunnies in a row and began looking for what was "out of place."

"They look the same to me!" said Giggles. "Same pants, same shirt, same floppy ears, and same silly smile!"

"They look the same to me, too!" said Lance. "Do you want me to roar and scare them into telling us which is the right rabbit?"

"No, no" said Chewy. "It's clear which rabbit is the one we should follow. Can't you see?"

And while it was clear to Chewy, it wasn't to the others.

"What's so different?" said Lance, impatiently.

"Their tails!" said Chewy.

"Their *tails!*" said the friends.

"That's right," he said. "Three hares have tails that are the wrong color. They're the out-of-place hares. But the real rabbit has a fluffy, cotton-white tail.

And Chewy was right.

Time was running out on a beautiful, adventure-filled day. So the four friends ran after the hare with the cotton-white tail until he came to a very tall fence.

The fence was like a very long wall with a giant-size gate. And hanging on the gate was the last, golden key.

"Yea, Chewy!" cried all the others. And they danced and jumped around like it was the last day of school before Christmas vacation.

It was the Lion's quick thinking and determined personality that won the first key. It was the Otter's joyful and hopeful ways which found the second. And the Golden Retriever's caring heart and listening ear had led them to the third key.

But it took a Beaver's careful attention to details to figure out what was different about those rabbits. And that's why Chewy was the one to find the final key.

But now how were the best friends going to use their four keys to reach the Treasure Tree?

"Keep your eyes focused on what is right. . . .
Be careful what you do. Always do what is right." —Proverbs

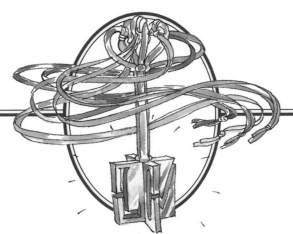

THE KEY
TO THE
TREASURE TREE

The four best friends had learned many things in their search for the Treasure Tree—especially how much they needed each other.

. . . It had taken the quick thinking of a determined Lion to get them across the Uncrossable River (and to put up with getting a pie on the head).

. . . It had taken an Otter's joyful and hopeful ways to find a key that none could see (and to rescue Chewy from the giant clam!).

. . . It had taken the Golden Retriever's caring heart and listening ears to hear the butterfly's cry for help (and keep her from becoming the spider's dinner).

. . . And it had taken a Beaver's close attention to detail to discover the out-of-place hares (and to see just how far an elephant's sneeze could take them).

Now, at last, they had come to the end of their journey—well, almost.

They could *see* the Treasure Tree! It was tall and strong like a beautiful oak tree. And it had delicious chocolate hearts wrapped in shiny red paper hanging from each branch. But . . . *the only way to the Treasure Tree was through the big locked gate!*

"We're here!" cried Lance! "We made it!"

"Let's go in," said Giggles. "I can't wait to taste those chocolates!"

"Our keys!" shouted Chewy. "Our *keys* must open the gate. That's why we had to search for them."

"Let's give them a try!" said Lance. He put his key into the big lock on the gate and turned the key. . . . But nothing happened.

"Let me try my key!" said Giggles. She put her key into the same hole, but it did not work either.

"Try mine!" said the Beaver. Still the gate did not open. Then Honey the Golden Retriever said, "It must be mine!" But it wasn't. They still couldn't get the gate to open!

Now the animals were stumped. They had come so far . . . gone through so much . . . gathered every key . . . and yet they still couldn't get the gate to open!

"How are we going to get in?" asked Honey. And that's when they heard a familiar voice.

"Don't worry, best friends," said Wise Old Owl. "You've got the key to unlock the gate right in your hands."

"What do you mean 'we've got the key to unlock the gate'?" said Lance, sounding a little cross. "We've tried all our keys and none of them works!"

"Ah, but you're missing something," said the Owl in a kind voice. "What was it that you learned on your adventures?"

"How to pick a blueberry pie. . . . How to tickle a clam. . . . How never to stand near an elephant when he's sneezing . . ." said the Otter.

"No, no, no . . ." said the Owl. "What did you learn about *each other?*"

The four best friends thought for a minute. Then finally, Honey the Golden Retriever spoke up.

"I think what you're trying to say is that we've already found the real treasure when we learned how much we need each other. We're all different in many ways, and that's why each of us was able to solve a different riddle. Is that it Wise Old Owl?"

It was.

"Then I know how to open the gate!" cried Chewy! (Leave it to Beaver to solve the last piece of the puzzle.) "Let's put our keys together. And when the four best friends put their four small keys together, they made one large key that fit perfectly into the lock.
Lance turned the keys, and the gate swung wide open.

The four best friends ran to the tree for the biggest chocolate feast ever. But the very best treasure of all was knowing how much they loved and needed each other!

106

And they would never forget the Wise Old Owl's final
words:

*"The greatest truth you'll learn today
Is friends need friends along the way."*

107

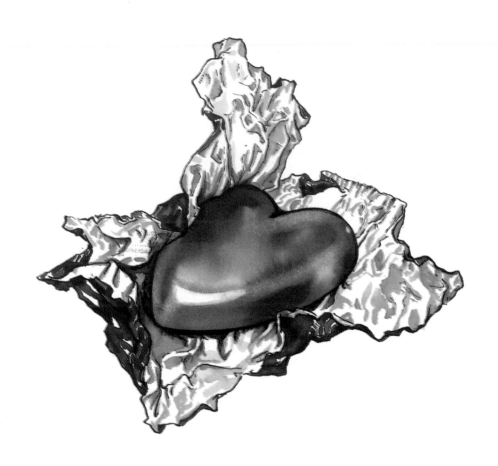

A FINAL WORD TO PARENTS

We hope you and your little one(s) have enjoyed reading *The Treasure Tree*. Like all authors, we hope the book entertained you. But, more than that, we hope it encouraged and even challenged you.

The four animals in this story came out of the personality section we teach in our "Love Is a Decision" seminars, based on our book *The Two Sides of Love*. Not only do we want children to begin to learn the different personality characteristics, but it is also our deep desire to help parents begin to recognize and highly value even their very young children's unique, God-given bents.

It was our good friend Chuck Swindoll who first pointed out to us how the familiar Proverb "Train up a child in the way he should go . . ." should best be translated. The way it actually reads in Hebrew is "Train up a child according to his bent. . . ."

We hope that by using four animals to describe the four basic personality types, we have helped you to see more clearly your child's "bent." And for you to help your child learn more about his own personality strengths, we've included a brief personality checklist for the two of you to do together.

The instructions are very easy. Simply circle the descriptions that show your child's consistent characteristics. Total the circles in each personality area, and you'll see your child's personality strengths. Is he a lion, an otter, a golden retriever, or a beaver?

As you learn more about your child in particular, learn to praise him in light of his God-given talents. If you're the parent of a child with a lion personality (who probably is allowing *you* to live in your home!), understanding his decisive, goal-driven nature can help you relate to him, not react to him.

Recognizing your Otter child's fun-loving nature, your Golden Retriever child's sensitive side, and your Beaver child's tendencies toward perfectionism can also be very helpful in coming up with a parenting plan.

For additional information on your child's personal strengths, we have just the resource for you. In fact, our book *The Two Sides of Love* was written specifically so that Lions and Beavers would learn to balance their love with softness, and that Otters and Golden Retrievers would learn to balance their love with strength.

And if your child seems to be a "pure-bred" lion, we recommend another resource for you. It's the book *Who's in Charge Here?* by our friend Dr. Robert Barnes.

May the Lord bless you as you read to your little one(s), snuggle them close, and affirm their God-given strengths.

John Trent, Ph.D., and Gary Smalley

PERSONALITY CHECKLIST

Read the following personality descriptions to your child, and let him pick the ones he thinks are most like him. Circle each description that is a consistent character trait of your child. Then total the circled answers for each personality. The larger numbers indicate basic personality traits.

LION:

1. Is daring and unafraid in new situations.
2. Likes to be a leader. Often tells others how to do things.
3. Ready to take on any kind of challenge.
4. Is firm and serious about what is expected.
5. Makes decisions quickly.

Total = _____

OTTER:

1. Talks a lot and tells wild stories.
2. Likes to do all kinds of fun things.
3. Enjoys being in groups. Likes to perform.
4. Full of energy and always eager to play.
5. Always happy and sees the good part of everything.

Total = _____

GOLDEN RETRIEVER:

1. Always loyal and faithful to friends.
2. Listens carefully to others.
3. Likes to help others. Feels sad when others are hurt.
4. Is a peacemaker. Doesn't like it when others argue.
5. Patient and willing to wait for something.

Total = _____

BEAVER:

1. Is neat and tidy and notices little details.
2. Sticks with something until it's done. Doesn't like to quit in the middle of a game.
3. Asks lots of questions.
4. Likes things done the same way.
5. Tells things just the way they are.

Total = _____